How to RAISE THREE DRAGONS

adapted by Ellie O'Ryan

Ready-to-Read

Simon Spotlight

New York   London   Toronto   Sydney   New Delhi

SIMON SPOTLIGHT
An imprint of Simon & Schuster Children's Publishing Division
1230 Avenue of the Americas, New York, New York 10020
This Simon Spotlight edition September 2015
DreamWorks Dragons © 2015 DreamWorks Animation LLC. All Rights Reserved.
All rights reserved, including the right of reproduction in whole or in part in any form.
SIMON SPOTLIGHT, READY-TO-READ, and colophon are registered trademarks of Simon & Schuster, Inc.
For information about special discounts for bulk purchases, please contact Simon & Schuster Special Sales at
1-866-506-1949 or business@simonandschuster.com.
Manufactured in the United States of America 0815 LAK
2 4 6 8 10 9 7 5 3 1
ISBN 978-1-4814-4123-0 (hc)
ISBN 978-1-4814-4122-3 (pbk)
ISBN 978-1-4814-4124-7 (eBook)

Hiccup's new invention,
the Thunder-Ear,
was finally ready.
He couldn't wait to test it!

Stoick had never seen anything
like the Thunder-Ear.
"It can track dragon sounds
from miles away," Hiccup explained.

Stoick leaned close to the
Thunder-Ear.
He heard Fishlegs and Meatlug
singing.
But they were very far away.
The Thunder-Ear worked!

Then Stoick heard something
even worse.
"Tell them to stop singing,"
he said.
But the terrible noise wasn't
Fishlegs and Meatlug.
It was three baby
Thunderdrum dragons!

Stoick's dragon, Thornado, was a Thunderdrum, too. He recognized their cries and zoomed off to find them. They were all by themselves on a sea stack.

Hiccup didn't want to leave
the baby Thunderdrums alone.
But Stoick said they were too loud
to live in the village.
"They'll be okay on their own," he
told Hiccup.
"Thunderdrums are the toughest
dragons in the world!"

At dawn the next morning Hiccup
jumped out of bed.
What was that terrible noise?
It was the Thunderdrum dragons!
They had followed Hiccup and Stoick
back to Berk.
And they were out of control!

The baby dragons
zoomed through houses,
crashed into food carts,
and even scared the sheep!

"Can you help me wrangle them
into the Academy?" Hiccup shouted.
"I thought you'd never ask!"
Astrid replied.

"Get those troublemakers off
the island now!" Stoick ordered,
once Thornado had calmed
the three baby Thunderdrums.
"Don't you think we should
train them?" Hiccup asked.

Stoick thought about it.
Thornado was a Thunderdrum,
and he was a great dragon.
Maybe the baby Thunderdrums
would be useful, too,
but only if Hiccup could train them.

"I guess the first thing we should do is name them!" Hiccup yelled.

The Thunderdrums were so loud that they drowned out everyone else!

The friends decided to call them
Bing, Bam, and Boom.
Noisy names for noisy dragons!

"Let's try some training,"
Hiccup said.
At first Bing, Bam, and Boom
did what Hiccup wanted.
But then the trouble started.

Bing, Bam, and Boom roared so loudly
that Hiccup flew across the arena.
When Astrid told them to stay,
they flew in circles.
Snotlout set up some targets,
but they knocked him down instead!
They even swiped Fishlegs' sword!

At last the Thunderdrums were calm.
"We're finally getting through
to them," said Hiccup.
But he was wrong.
It wasn't the training that
made the Thunderdrums behave.
It was Thornado!

Bing, Bam, and Boom were
perfectly behaved with Thornado.
They wanted to be just like him.
And when Thornado flew out of the
arena, the babies followed him!
"Close the gates!" yelled Hiccup.
But it was too late!

Once more Bing, Bam, and Boom
raced through the village.
They shrieked, roared,
and wrecked everything!

"The Thunderdrums have to go," Stoick ordered.

Everyone worked together to bring
Bing, Bam, and Boom
to a new home on Dragon Island.
"Here you can be as loud as you want,"
Hiccup told them.
"It will be great!"

Then Hiccup, Toothless, and the others flew away from Dragon Island. Far below, the baby Thunderdrums looked as sad as Hiccup felt.

Back at the village Hiccup found
a big surprise.
Bing, Bam, and Boom had
followed him home again.

Stoick was not happy to see Bing, Bam, and Boom.

"It looks like Thornado and I need to give you a hand," he told Hiccup.

Thornado led the baby Thunderdrums
back to Dragon Island.
Hiccup and Fishlegs followed
on their dragons.

Hiccup said good-bye
to Bing, Bam, and Boom again.
They started to cry.
That made Hiccup feel even worse.

"Don't look back, son," Stoick said
as they flew away.
But when Hiccup heard a scary roar,
he had to see what was happening.

A pack of wild dragons surrounded
Bing, Bam, and Boom!
"We're not going to let any wild
dragons bully our boys, are we?"
Stoick yelled.

Thornado and the other dragons
raced back to Dragon Island.
Then Thornado used his roar
to scare the wild dragons away.
Toothless and Meatlug helped too!

At last the baby Thunderdrums
were safe!
But what if the wild dragons
came back?
Bing, Bam, and Boom were too young
to be alone.
Stoick knew what he had to do.

Stoick removed Thornado's saddle.
"Take care of your new family,"
he said. "Good-bye, old friend."
It wasn't easy to say good-bye,
but Stoick knew it was right.
Thornado was a great dragon,
and now he would be a great dad!